CIRCUS

Lois Ehlert

HarperCollins*Publishers*

Ladies and gentlemen!

Welcome to the

greatest circus on earth.

Please take your seats.

First Edition
Library of Congress
Cataloging-in-Publication Data
Ehlert, Lois.
Circus / Lois Ehlert.
p.   cm.
Summary: Leaping lizards, march-
ing snakes, a bear on the high
wire, and others perform in
a somewhat unusual circus.
ISBN 0-06-020252-1
ISBN 0-06-020253-X (lib. bdg.)
(1. Circus—Fiction.
2. Animals—Fiction.) I. Title.
PZ7.E3225Ci   1992
(E)—dc20   91-12067
                    CIP
                    AC

Let's begin our show
with Hugo,
the world's biggest
elephant.

Captured
in the wild,
he's truly a mighty,
massive mammoth.

For our next act,
please welcome
the daring darling
of our show,
Princess Lydia,

as she rides bareback
on her prancing horse.

Now,
let's hear
a little applause
for Fritz
the wonder bear
as he rides
on the high wire.

Look, no paws!

Hold your breath
and cross your fingers
as those marvelous
musclemen,
the Pretzel
brothers,
form a
towering
human
pyramid.

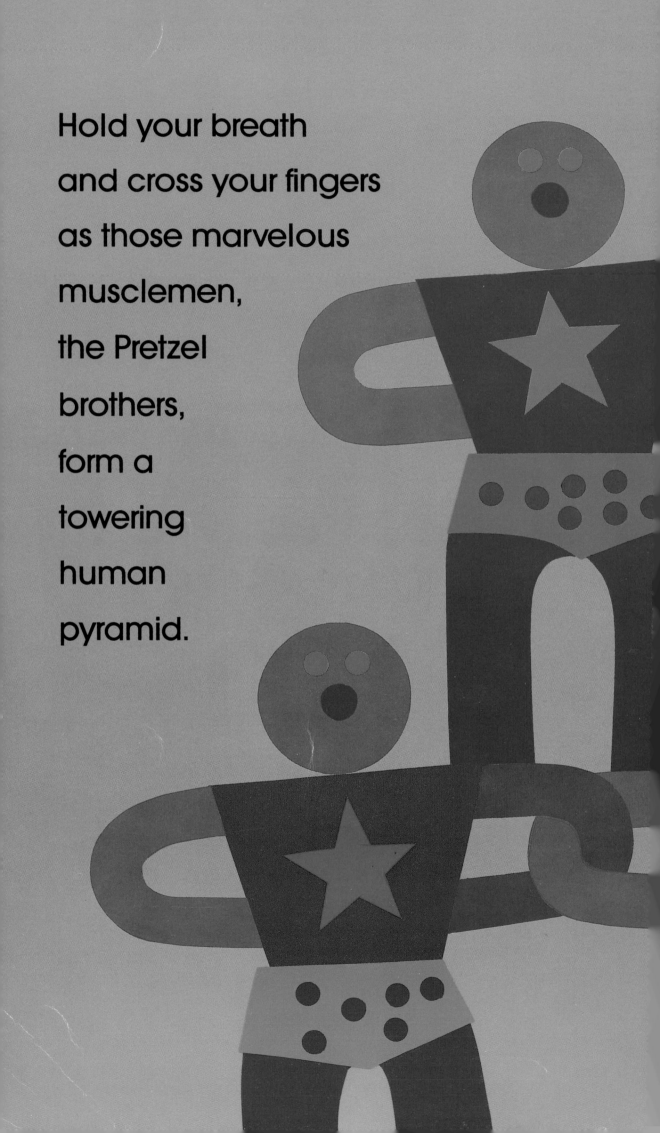

Watch closely as Samu,

the fiercest tiger in the world,

jumps through a flaming hoop.

It's amazing, isn't it, folks?

Ladies and gentlemen!

It's time for a short intermission.

We'll be right back.

Get
your
cotton
candy,

snow
cones
here.

Hungry?
Thirsty?
Step
right
up.

Popcorn,
peanuts,
ice cream
bars.

Hot dogs,
soda,
souvenirs.

Welcome back, folks.
On with the show!

I'm proud to present
Lena and Lila, the fearless
leaping lizards.

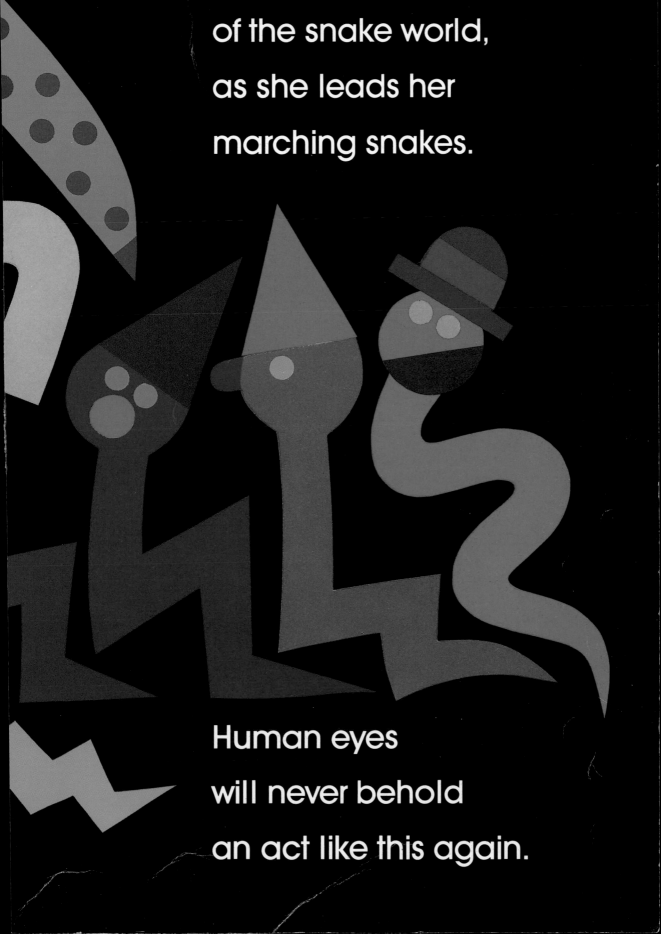

And now,

back by popular demand,

Buster and Buck,

the world-famous goats.

Please,
my friends,
a moment of silence, as the
flying Zucchinis attempt
a twisting triple somersault.

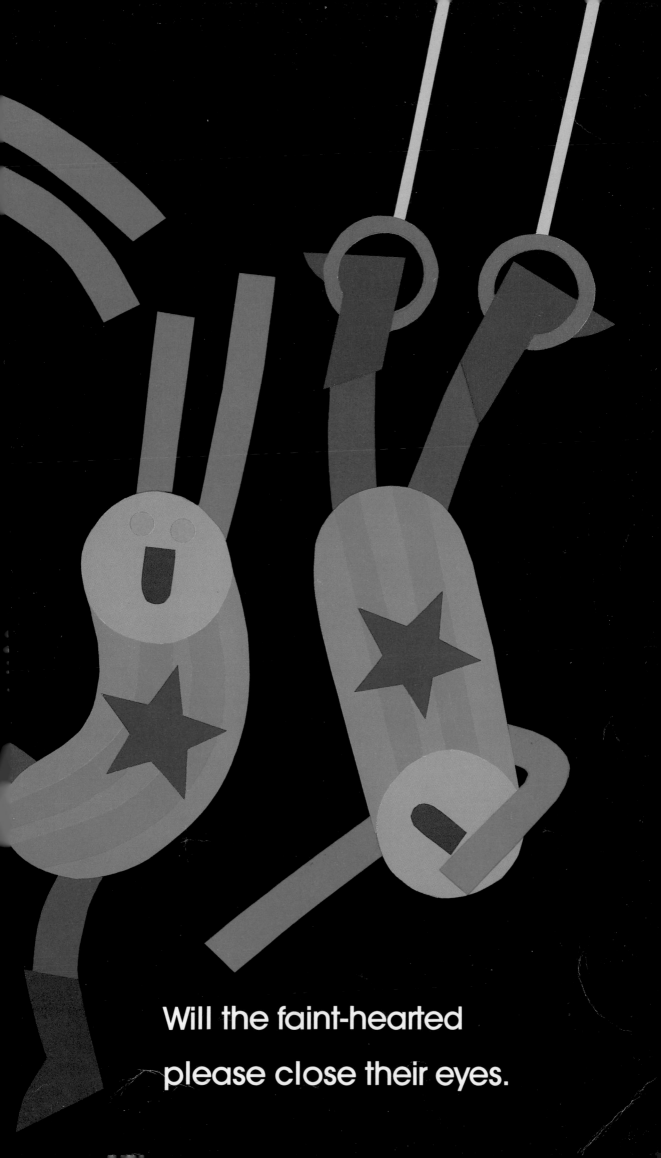

Will the faint-hearted
please close their eyes.

Sit back and relax now
as beautiful Bertha and her
rainbow parrots whistle
"Twinkle, Twinkle,
Little Star."

And now, for our final act,
Bruno the magnificent
dares to place his head
in the jaws of a
ferocious lion!

Please remain calm.
Loud noise makes the lion jumpy.

That's
the end
of our show,
folks!

Let's give
everybody
a big hand.

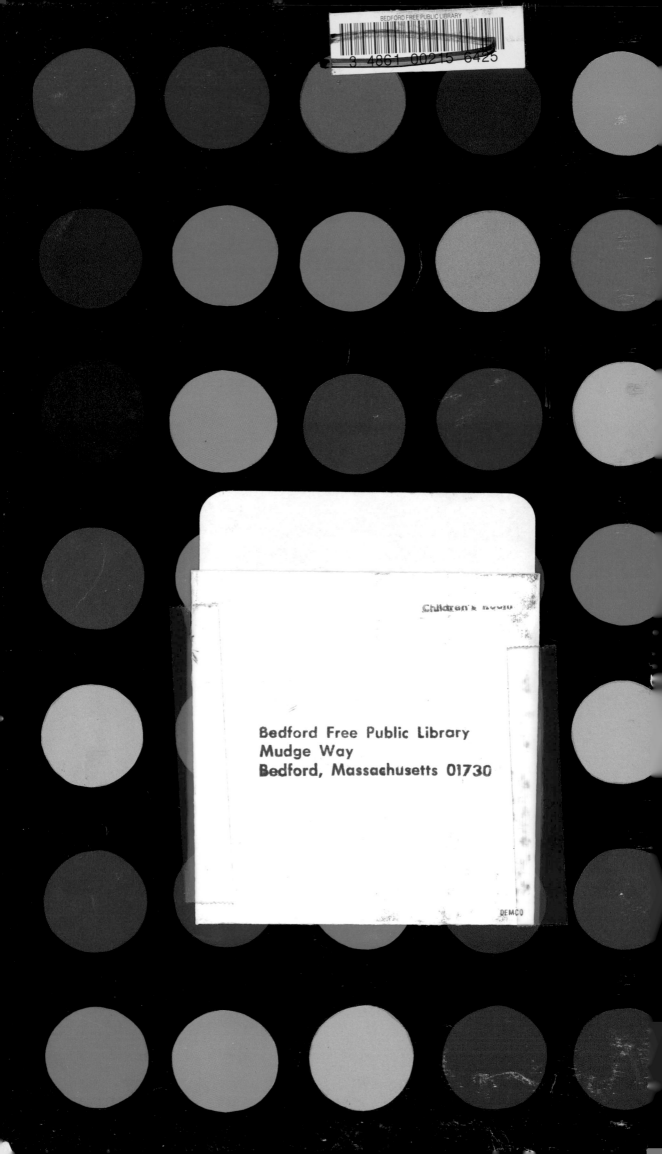